DRUMMER HOFF

DRUMMER HOFF

Adapted by Barbara Emberley   Illustrated by Ed Emberley

Prentice-Hall, Inc., Englewood Cliffs, N. J.

DRUMMER HOFF   By Ed and Barbara Emberley   © 1967 by Edward R. Emberley and Barbara Emberley.
0-13-220855-5(pbk.); 0-13-220822-9

20   19   18   17   16   15   14   13   12

Drummer Hoff fired it off.

Private Parriage
brought the carriage,

but Drummer Hoff fired it off.

Corporal Farrell
brought the barrel.

Corporal Farrell
brought the barrel,
Private Parriage
brought the carriage,
but Drummer Hoff
fired it off.

Sergeant Chowder
brought the powder.

Sergeant Chowder
brought the powder,
Corporal Farrell
brought the barrel,
Private Parriage
brought the carriage,
but Drummer Hoff
fired it off.

Captain Bammer
brought the rammer.

Captain Bammer
brought the rammer,
Sergeant Chowder
brought the powder,
Corporal Farrell
brought the barrel,
Private Parriage
brought the carriage,
but Drummer Hoff fired it off.

Major Scott
brought the shot.

Major Scott brought the shot,
Captain Bammer
brought the rammer,
Sergeant Chowder
brought the powder,
Corporal Farrell
brought the barrel,
Private Parriage
brought the carriage,
but Drummer Hoff fired it off.

General Border
gave the order.

General Border
gave the order,
Major Scott
brought the shot,
Captain Bammer
brought the rammer,
Sergeant Chowder
brought the powder,
Corporal Farrell
brought the barrel,
Private Parriage
brought the carriage,
but Drummer Hoff fired it off.